PRAISE FOR M. L. BUCHMAN

Top 10 Romance of 2012, 2015, and 2016.

— BOOKLIST: THE NIGHT IS MINE, HOT POINT, HEART STRIKE

One of our favorite authors.

— RT BOOK REVIEWS

Buchman has catapulted his way to the top tier of my favorite authors.

— FRESH FICTION

A favorite author of mine. I'll read anything that carries his name, no questions asked. Meet your new favorite author!

— THE SASSY BOOKSTER, FLASH OF FIRE

M.L. Buchman is guaranteed to get me lost in a good story.

— THE READING CAFE, WAY OF THE WARRIOR: NSDQ

I love Buchman's writing. His vivid descriptions
bring everything to life in an unforgettable way.

— PURE JONEL, HOT POINT

THEY'D MOST CERTAINLY BE FLYING

AN OREGON FIREBIRDS ROMANCE

M. L. BUCHMAN

Buchman Bookworks

Receive a free book and discover more by this author at:
www.mlbuchman.com

Cover images:

Firefighting helicopter © carlosmoura

Young couple quarreling isolated on white background © pio3

SIGN UP FOR M. L. BUCHMAN'S
NEWSLETTER TODAY

and receive:
Release News
Free Short Stories
a Free book

Do it today. Do it now.
http://free-book.mlbuchman.com

Other works by M. L. Buchman:

The Night Stalkers

Main Flight

The Night Is Mine
I Own the Dawn
Wait Until Dark
Take Over at Midnight
Light Up the Night
Bring On the Dusk
By Break of Day

White House Holiday

Daniel's Christmas
Frank's Independence Day
Peter's Christmas
Zachary's Christmas
Roy's Independence Day
Damien's Christmas

and the Navy

Christmas at Steel Beach
Christmas at Peleliu Cove

5E

Target of the Heart
Target Lock on Love
Target of Mine

Firehawks

Main Flight

Pure Heat
Full Blaze
Hot Point
Flash of Fire
Wild Fire

Smokejumpers

Wildfire at Dawn
Wildfire at Larch Creek
Wildfire on the Skagit

Delta Force

Target Engaged
Heart Strike
Wild Justice

Where Dreams

Where Dreams are Born
Where Dreams Reside
Where Dreams Are of Christmas
Where Dreams Unfold
Where Dreams Are Written

Eagle Cove

Return to Eagle Cove
Recipe for Eagle Cove
Longing for Eagle Cove
Keepsake for Eagle Cove

Henderson's Ranch

Nathan's Big Sky

Love Abroad

Heart of the Cotswolds: England

Dead Chef Thrillers

Swap Out!
One Chef!
Two Chef!

Deities Anonymous

Cookbook from Hell: Reheated
Saviors 101

SF/F Titles

The Nara Reaction
Monk's Maze
the Me and Elsie Chronicles

Strategies for Success (NF)

Managing Your Inner Artist/Writer
Estate Planning for Authors

"*What* kind of a heap is that?"

Stacy looked up at the man climbing out of the car next to hers. He'd been riding her bumper since she'd pulled out of Cave Junction, Oregon five miles back. The tighter he'd hung in his black classic Pontiac Firebird Trans Am, the slower she went in her not so classic 1993 Toyota extended cab pickup. They'd barely been crawling when they reached the dusty Illinois Valley Airport parking lot.

He was a big guy—in a multi-muscle way: muscle car, seriously muscled chest under his tight University of Washington Huskies t-shirt, and a total musclehead. His dark wrap-around shades were as retro as his ride.

"My kind of heap. How many miles do you have on that Firebird?"

He grinned down at his car like it was a beloved pet. "Just seventy-five thou. Ain't she sweet?"

"And *she'll* be on the junk heap before a hundred and fifty. Unless," she made a guess, "you replace the engine...*again*."

He scowled that she'd nailed it. Not hard, as it was a high odds bet that the miles he'd put on it hadn't been easy ones.

"I've already got three-hundred thousand on my *heap's* original engine."

His scowl darkened even more.

Maybe if she waited long enough, he'd move one step closer and she could take him out at the knees with her truck's door. It was low enough on the little half-ton pickup. The truck had been a gift from her big brother, Bill, before he'd been blown up in a "training exercise in Alabama"—except she knew he'd been in Iraq and his death was accompanied by two new medals. They didn't give those kinds of medals for training accidents. It was all she had left of him other than a folded flag and his dog tags.

"What are you doing here, honey? You lost?" The guy asked her in his best demeaning tone.

"What are *you* doing here… Oh, wait. Never mind. I already know."

"What's that?"

"Being an asshole for a living."

Instead of going to fury—she'd quietly put her truck in reverse and was ready to pop the clutch and peel out if necessary—he grinned. "Most folks don't know that about me."

"Seemed pretty damn obvious from where I'm sitting."

He burst out a laugh. It was a big one that seemed to fill the air—which definitely needed something. The April morning was already hot and dry.

The small airport was five miles south of Cave Junction, which wasn't much of a town by anyone's standards except rural Oregon's. Two thousand people and six restaurants—if you counted the Dutch Bros. Coffee drive through—were tucked in the rough terrain close by the California border. The closest town that was any bigger was Grants Pass, over thirty miles back. There was an aridness to the land here that seemed wrong after growing up farther up the coast. Around here, the Douglas firs were scattered rather than growing in thick, mountain-covering expanses. Tall grasses predominated, which would be dangerously dry and brown long before fire season. Even more so around the airport: a flat, baking expanse with no activity beneath the blazing sunshine other than this two-legged laughing hyena.

"Enjoying yourself?"

"Immensely," he was still grinning.

She told herself not to, but was weak and asked, "Why?"

"Because I just figured out who you are."

"You mean other than a pain in the ass." She'd been called that enough times in her life to bury a multitude of lesser sins.

"Yep! Other than that. You're Stacy Richardson and you're here to fly helicopters."

Only one man would know that. Curt Williams—her new boss… Who she'd just called an asshole.

Stacy sighed and climbed out of her truck. At least she was batting her usual average.

2

Curt was glad for the dark glasses, so that he could take a moment and really look at the woman. His big sister had sent Stacy his way. Jana was a former heli-pilot for the 101st Airborne and was the logistics arm of their new business, the Oregon Firebirds. She may have lost a hand during a stupid accident while serving in Okinawa, but it didn't diminish her flying smarts a bit.

She'd kicked him a text, "I hired you a pilot. Stacy Richardson is an even better flyer than you."

Women were still rare in the helicopter world, so he'd assumed Stacy was a guy. He wouldn't put it past his sister knowing that for a second. He'd ignore the last part of the message as mere sibling harassment.

Stacy was definitely way better *looking* than he was though. Half a head shorter, trim of waist, but the ranting Donald Duck on her Oregon State University Ducks t-shirt was definitely nicely stretched. She had long dark hair that fell past her shoulders in soft waves tangled by the wind of driving with her window down. The sun caught red highlights and made her shine. Her aviator shades hid her eyes but not her thoughts.

"Huskies. Oh, my, God! I can't believe that I signed on to work for a Washington Husky fan."

"Beats the Ducks any day."

"And which football team had a twelve-year winning streak over the Huskies? Oh wait, it was the Ducks."

"Which was ended. By the Huskies."

"For the moment. I don't know why you guys even bother showing up. Ducks are gonna wipe the field with you something fierce come fall." And Curt hoped that the second part of Jana's message *was* just exaggeration. Being humbled by a Duck in the air would be a sad state of affairs. Searching for another topic, he looked down at her battered little pickup. The backseat appeared to be crammed with a hodgepodge of belongings. The truck bed had a low cap on it, the same height as the cab. For a moment, it seemed that her whole life was parked right here in front of him just waiting to be discovered.

"You do get that you're going to be flying for the *Firebirds.*" He needed something else to think about because the more he looked at her, the more he saw to like. Good muscle tone, hard-worn running shoes, and an open stance that didn't include the least bit of cowed.

"And your point is?"

With perfect timing, Jasper and a line of the three other pilots who'd be flying with him and Stacy raced into the parking lot. They swooped off the Redwood Highway at high speed, each unleashing a spray of gravel as they slid to a halt: a standard Firebird, a Camaro, and a pair of GTOs. All painted either red, or black with red flames—though none as cool as the Firebird painted on his own black hood.

"What's with the pickup?" Jasper asked as he climbed

out of the lead car. "Got us another hot chick mechanic? Way to go, Curt."

"That's my point," Curt told Stacy pointing at the line of cars.

"What? That you hire assholes like you?" But she backed it up with a grin that said she understood he was talking about the cars and was game to take them all on. He could get to like that in the woman.

"Naw," he turned to Jasper and the other guys. "Sis says she's gonna fly the pants off us." He could feel the eyeroll from Stacy at his word choice.

"Sounds like a good contest to me," Jasper tugged on a white cowboy hat.

"Only if you like walking around in just your tighty-whities and a cowboy hat," Stacy shot back at him. She might be a slim-and-trim cutie, but she clearly didn't take shit from anybody and Curt definitely liked that.

"Let's find out," he nodded up the road toward the line of pickups that had followed his crew at a barely more sedate pace.

Stacy had been flying to fire for various outfits for over five years and knew what to expect from guys.

Cowboy Hat and the other three new arrivals were predictably male, but she was having trouble pegging Curt Williams. One moment he was being true-to-expectations Mr. Macho Jerk, and other moments he appeared to be giving her the benefit of the doubt—which was rare enough in the general male pilot population to be exceptional.

She turned to look up the road where Curt had indicated and spotted a line of three big GMC Denali 3500 pickups with rear dualies. They were serious overkill, but they were very pretty. They could haul far more load than the two helicopters they each had under wraps on a flatbed trailer.

Jana Williams drove the first truck. She was the one who'd taken her up on a test flight over in Bend. She was a sharp contrast to her brother—a serious blonde who kept her thoughts to herself. A man and a woman drove the other two trucks that pulled in to line up on the dirt of the parking area as neat as a line of kites flying from the same string.

Illinois Valley Airport had been the Siskiyou Smokejumper Base and launched teams to fifteen hundred fires from the 1940s through the '80s. Now it was a sleepy, nowhere place without even a restaurant.

"Heart of fire country," Jana had told her during the interview. "And cheap. We like cheap."

There was nothing cheap about the rigs as everyone pitched in to unwrap and assemble the helos. Not only not cheap, but all of it looked factory new. There was serious money behind the outfit, which Jana had proven with the very generous offer that had bought her away from Columbia Helicopters.

The six brilliantly red **MD 520N NOTAR** helicopters were small, agile craft with impressive power for their size. They were notoriously tough machines, a variant of the ones used by the Night Stalkers her brother had flown for. The NOTAR—short for No Tail Rotor—was a quieter and safer version of the 520. The tail rotor was replaced by a high speed fan to counteract the main rotor's torque. Instead of using a four-blade rear rotor that always seemed to be begging to be taken out by flying debris, the fan simply drove air sideways out of a variable port to counteract the spin. Also, walking into the 520N's low tail wouldn't chop you into little pieces as there were no spinning parts.

Stacy ran her hand over the side of the aircraft. It *was* brand new and completely beautiful.

Just like a military bird, it had her name painted on the side. The Firebirds hadn't merely hired her to fly; they'd hired her to stay. A bonus that Jana hadn't mentioned.

She looked over at Curt, but he was busy with Jasper

swinging out the blades on another helo. The blades had been lashed in line with the tail booms for transport. Somehow she knew that putting the pilots' names on their aircraft had been his doing, not his sister's. Jana didn't strike her as the kind of woman who cared about such niceties—Stacy was surprised to discover that she herself was.

She touched her brother's dog tags where they hung down inside her shirt. They'd soon be flying together just like they had as teens when he'd taught her his own passion for rotorcraft. Their family still had a tourist business flying a helo farther up the coast—a sideline that never did more than break even for her father's farm.

Why any sane person would farm in Otis, Oregon was beyond her. Just because great-granddad had been dumb enough to buy land there using his GI bill money from WWII, didn't mean that they had to stay. It received eight feet, over ninety inches, of rain a year. It ranked eighth in the entire country for days with precipitation. It was a wonder she hadn't drowned as a child. It was also no surprise that both of her parents were alcoholics. Thankfully they were quiet, depressive drunks, but still.

But she'd survived, both the drowning rain and her drowning parents. All thanks to her brother. Bill had taught her how to fly. She'd actually paid for college by flying in the summers. She'd go land near the tourist beaches and put out a banner for sightseeing flights. Dad hadn't cared as long as she took care of fuel and maintenance. It was the only years of success for Richardson helicopters.

Now she didn't know why she'd wasted the time and money. Not the flying, but the college. A degree in political science had seemed practical. Following in her brother's footsteps…until one day his dog tags had come home without him. She'd finished her last semester, though she didn't remember any of it, and then she'd flown. Somewhere in the air over a Montana fire she'd come to— as if she'd spent the last six months asleep. Already doing what she'd been meant to do.

"Gonna just stand there and admire it all day?" Curt had come up beside her without her noticing. His words were teasing, but his tone was kind.

"Thank you for my name," she rubbed a hand over the letters again, barely able to feel the raised surface of the gloss paint.

"It's what a pilot deserves."

She looked up at the wistful tone in his voice.

He tapped one ear, "Mostly deaf on this side. All that kept me from following my sister into the Army. Fine for commercial flying though."

"Bill, my—" but the words choked off on her and she had to look away. She ran her hand over the helicopter's smooth skin again. "Thank you for both of us."

---

4

*C*urt didn't know what to say to that. There was
pain there. And love. He could hear it and it
humbled him. He loved his sister, he supposed. Yeah, sure
he did. Because brothers loved their sisters, even if they
made you batshit crazy half the time just by being alive
and drawing breath. But he'd never found anything that
would sound like that simple "thank you" did in Stacy
Richardson's soft voice.

In silence, he'd helped her roll the helo off the trailer.

They had three of the five rotor blades rigged before
the silence built to the point where he couldn't stand it any
more. He started babbling about his business plans. He,
Jasper, and Jana had worked them out together.

"There's that big outfit up in northern Oregon, Mount
Hood Aviation. They fly all these big aircraft, Firehawks
and even an Erickson Aircrane. I can loft all six of these
520s for the cost of one of their Firehawks. I could launch
ten for the price of their Aircrane. I figure that with the
pickup trucks for transport, we can be almost anywhere in
the West within a day. And the 520s let us tackle fires in a

way that matters to the insurance companies even more than the Forest Service."

"Saving structures."

"Bingo." He liked that Stacy saw it right away. "With a line of six of these little babies, we can get up close and personal with spot fires before they can kill off a structure. We're set up at a discount with the Forest Service so that we get early call to fires and an insurance bonus for every structure we save. Hence the cameras," he pointed underneath. Everything would be videoed and then submitted to insurers as proof for each time they saved a million-dollar home, or a hundred-dollar shed. As far as he knew, it was a first-ever business set up this way and he could only hope that it worked, because he and his sister had gambled everything on it.

They were hocked up to their eyeballs. He hated to do so, but he prayed for a busy fire season. Because if it was a slow one, the Oregon Firebirds weren't likely to see another.

Stacy nodded as if it all made sense to her. More than the financial scheme. As if she could see the dreams and sweat of the last three years putting together the right deals, the right gear, and the right people.

Now why was her approval so important to him? It was like a sigh of relief went through him that it would all somehow work even if smart money said otherwise.

They swung the last blade into place as the fuel truck finished topping up the tank.

She took a moment to glance around the field.

He followed her gaze. Everyone looked ready.

Then she turned to him and smiled. It lit her up. She was already beautiful, but damn that smile was electric.

"So, shall we see who gets to keep their pants on?"

Suddenly Curt wasn't so sure that he wanted to compete against her in a flight.

Ten hours later, sitting down around the firepit with the other fliers, he knew he'd never risk underestimating her again. After a day of working on shakedowns and team coordination, there was no longer any question about who was the hotshot pilot of the outfit. There wasn't a single guy here who shouldn't be down to his skivvies.

5

"Something bothering you?" Jana asked as the three of them were settling into their bunks after another impossibly long firefight—their fourth major fire in five weeks. It felt good to be back at Illinois Valley Airport even if they'd been on the road more than they'd been here.

The bunkroom wasn't generous; it was best if they didn't all try to get dressed at the same time. Jana had the single bed on one wall. Maggie—their ace mechanic—had the top bunk above Stacy's lower. After the long drive back from the Idaho Trickle Creek Fire, which hadn't been trickling at all, she was too tired to even think.

"Sure," Stacy mumbled. "I'm desperate to know how long we actually get to stretch out on a crappy bunk before the next fire."

"Hey," Maggie stuck out her head and look down at her, temporarily blocking the too bright overhead light that no one had the energy to switch off. The shadows completely hid her expression. "I tightened the springs and put in a new board and everything."

"Sorry. Didn't mean to trigger the perfectionist in the room."

"Look who's talking," Maggie's silhouette rolled back out of sight.

Stacy considered rolling over to get out of the light, but just threw an arm over her face instead.

"We got us a trio of perfectionists in this bunkroom. Now if someone could explain the trash in those other two bunkhouses, that might help some."

"They're men. I guess we need to cut them some slack." Not that they'd been working one minute less than the women on the team.

When they had all first practiced together, it soon became apparent that Jana and Curt had assembled a very skilled group of pilots. But that wasn't enough for them as they'd conceived something grander.

In her experience most outfits debriefed the fire's behavior after each flight. The Firebirds debriefed aerial tactics. And it was paying off. On the first fire, a controlled burn over in Corvallis that had run out of control, they'd beaten and battered at the fire. Each MD 520N could deliver a half-ton of water—two hundred gallons—out of the belly tanks rigged between their skids. Curt had even spent the extra for deployable snorkels, so that they didn't have to land to retank, but could just hover over a stream or lake and refill in thirty seconds. If a retardant truck was handy, they could also land and refill in not many seconds more. But they'd made six separate attacks, fighting the fire in too many places at once.

Now, five hard weeks later, they attacked the fire in a tight line bunched like hydroplanes at the start of a race on Devil's Lake in Lincoln City. They focused on one house at a time. There was no way for their six little helos to stop the main front of a raging wildfire. But first they'd learned how to hold it back around a single house. Then they'd advanced. Rather than stopping the fire, they punched holes in it—holes that expanded to gaps. More than once, they'd saved a whole row of houses with the fencelines scorched out between them, but the structures still standing. Ka-ching! That's what they got paid for.

Doing it on their first big fire this week over in Idaho had confused the crap out of the air bosses. They'd had to fight tooth-and-nail to prove that their tactics were saving more homes, even at the cost of more forest. They'd finally convinced that one guy, but the next fire was probably going to be the same battle all over again. It was too exhausting to even think about.

Stacy's body was buzzing with that exhaustion so there was no way she was going to get to sleep.

"I need a beer," not that it would help, but it was better than lying here and not sleeping while her body buzzed.

"Something other than camp food," Jana sighed. "Like…pizza!"

"Men," Maggie groaned from the upper bunk. "We definitely need men."

"We've already got a supply of those," Stacy could feel them in the small huts next door.

"No. Those are our men. We need real ones. The kind we can be stupid about and not regret it in the morning."

There was a sudden silence as Stacy glanced over at Jana.

"Beer," she whispered.

"Pizza," Jana sat up enough to look at her.

"Men," Maggie again leaned out enough to block the light with her head.

"Road trip!" They all said it in unison.

"Shh!" Maggie made the sound far more loudly than

they'd been speaking. "Let's sneak. Otherwise our men will follow us and spoil the fun."

Jana dressed in nice slacks and a pretty blouse, a bright scrunchy hanked her long blonde hair into a ponytail.

"You're not going to wear your cosmetic hand?" Stacy had seen it in the drawer, because there was no privacy in a room this small. Come to think of it, she'd never seen Jana wearing anything but the hooks.

"I can drink beer and eat pizza with this one," she flexed a shoulder and clicked the opposing hooks together to emphasize her point. "If a guy can't deal with it, to hell with him."

"To hell with him," Maggie agreed cheerfully and Stacy echoed the sentiment.

Yes, to hell with him, whoever *him* was. Keeping that in mind, Stacy rehung her one fine change of clothes in the tiny closet. Instead she went with her standard Oregon attire: jeans with no char spots, a red t-shirt that said "Fire pilots are like fire, too hot to touch!", and a fleece REI shirt that covered most of the words. She tossed her hair over her shoulder and she was done.

Maggie changed into lacy red underwear—"In case I actually get lucky"—and then a low cut, clingy dress of flirty gold that offset her dark skin so that it looked like she was both glowing and perhaps a little evil. The hem landed well above her knees and pretty much guaranteed her luck if there was a single man anywhere in a dozen miles. She was also pixie high and by far the cutest of the three of them, so she and Jana wouldn't stand a chance until Maggie had her pick. Which was fine, Stacy wanted a beer. She might be tempted by a pizza, but men were nowhere on her list. Not until she found one with an ego smaller than a gray whale migrating up the coast. Not gonna happen on a fire line.

They slipped out the back, climbed into Stacy's little Toyota because they were all sick of riding back from Idaho in the big GMC Denali pickups. Maggie slipped into one of the small backseats that had her sitting sideways and they were off.

Jana turned to the only radio station that reached this far into the hills. They were playing *Boondocks* by Little Big Town. Definitely where they were. They sang along all the way into town.

6

Unable to sleep, Curt had tried to slip out, but Jasper had caught up with him in the parking lot. They'd been hanging together since they were teenagers dreaming of hot cars and chasing girls, or was it chasing cars and dreaming of hot girls. Their moods were so in sync, that it wasn't like he was following—if one went somewhere, of course the other one did as well.

The other three pilots, Drew, Amos, and Palo, were still sacked out.

They'd run into Ty mucking the road trip food wrappers and soda cans out of the trucks. "In case we get a call up tomorrow." He was the camp handyman, cook, and receptionist. Also Jana's right hand in training as well as helping Maggie with anything that took two people to fix. Ty chose to sack out rather than join them.

He and Jasper had just driven with no real destination in mind. They'd stumbled on Wild River Pizza in Cave Junction and pulled in. He parked his Trans Am in a shadowed corner so that no one would park next to it and give him a door ding.

They were sitting and watching the local talent, pretty thin on a Thursday night except for some tourists out to visit the Oregon Caves.

"Five weeks. Haven't seen the caves yet."

"Five weeks," Jasper agreed as he tipped his chair back on two legs. "Haven't seen much of anything except fire."

"Good thing," Curt propped his feet on an empty chair across the table.

"Keeping us busy."

"Keeping us paid."

They watched a couple playing pool. There was a nice view as the girl bent over to take a reaching shot. Not bad either when she stood up and did a little happy dance at sinking her ball. The guy standing beside her congratulated her with a kiss that looked very welcome.

"Yep," Jasper observed.

"Yep," Curt agreed. There was such a thing as being too damn busy, even if it was a good thing. The front door banged open and a trio of women strode in. There was a bright light making it hard to see their faces, but the rest of what showed was very fine. Their laughter brightened the sleepy bar.

"Huh," Jasper noted that the prospects for the night had just picked up.

Then the cheery trio stepped past the light and into clear view.

"Huh," Curt slouched down in his seat. Nothing happening, it was the Firebird women. Maggie did look hot, but that wasn't a real surprise—she always abounded with energy, though who knew she had legs like that. And enough deeply bronzed cleavage that…

That… Nothing! She was his mechanic. Besides, he knew that Drew and Amos were both all hot and bothered over her. Definitely didn't want to step into that mess. Still, tonight Maggie was a way hotter and sexier version of herself than he'd even guessed. He couldn't wait to rub it in that Drew and Amos both slept through the whole thing.

Jana too was transformed by dressing up—a major rarity for his sister—and had pulled her hair back. She normally wore it half covering her face. The legs of Jasper's chair thumped down onto the floor. He never spoke to Jana. One of these days, Curt would have to ask what he had against her.

But not tonight, because that's when Stacy stepped clear of his sister.

She looked…perfect.

He couldn't look away from her because she was so wholly unchanged. She was herself right to the core. The only thing she'd altered was wearing her hair down rather than in a ponytail. Damn but the woman had glorious hair.

Jasper tugged his cowboy hat lower until he might have not been able to see them at all.

Curt thought about it, then tugged his red Firebird billed hat lower, but not so low that he couldn't keep at least one eye on Stacy. Moving up to the bar, the women took stools. In moments they had beers and were flirting with the barman.

"Think we can slip away safe?" Jasper whispered from under his hat, though his head was cocked to watch the three women.

"Run or stay?"

"Run. Definitely." All six-three of Jasper was in danger of disappearing completely under his hat.

Best friend said "run," it was probably good advice. He

dug out a twenty and was about to toss it on the table when his sister looked into the angled mirror over the bar and glared right at him. After a long moment she mouthed something at him, so distinctly that he couldn't misread it.

"Chicken," Jana said loudly enough for Stacy to hear but not enough to interrupt Maggie's flirtation with the cute bartender.

"Why? Because I wouldn't answer your question earlier? Fine. Nothing's bothering me that three days of sleep wouldn't fix."

Jana turned to her from contemplating the mirror over the bar. "How long have we known each other?"

"A flight and an interview longer than anyone else in this outfit."

"That means I know you better than any of them."

Stacy considered. Then she raised her beer and clinked the already half empty glass against Jana's mostly full one —way fast for her. "First one I've shared a beer with. Does that make us best friends?"

That earned her a cool look and she wondered if Jana was the sort of woman to have best friends. Stacy liked her well enough—and respected the hell out of her competency—but friends might be a bit of a stretch.

"Beer's talking," she swallowed back some more to

make her point. She'd never had more than two since the day she'd understood that her parents were both alcoholics, never wanted more either, so she was safe.

"I'd say it makes me friend enough to call bullshit on your, 'Nothing's bothering me' pitch."

"But nothing is, other than how good a pilot you are. I've learned more about holes in my technique from you than I think I knew in total before meeting you."

Jana smiled sadly at that. "If I still had my hand, I'd take you up and show you some real 101st Airborne shit."

Stacy had almost stopped seeing the hooks that served Jana as her right hand.

"Anyway, I'm still calling bullshit on you."

"Why?" Stacy couldn't think of anything really bothering her.

Jana just nodded upward.

Stacy went to empty the dregs of her beer as she looked up into the mirror…and almost choked when she saw Curt standing just a step behind her.

8

Maggie had found a couple of retired Navy buddies, traveling with their wives. The five of them were talking Navy jets and RVs. Curt knew from long experience that anything with an engine earned a hundred percent of Maggie's attention no matter how she was dressed.

Jasper and Jana were playing a silent pool game with a grim determination that was actually a little freaky. The remains of a demolished beef, mushroom, and onion large-size pizza was spread across four plates, with a couple slices going over to Maggie.

Stacy sat across the table from him, leaning forward with an intensity that he'd wager wasn't going to make it to the bottom of her second beer. He liked that she was a total lightweight. It fit her far better than a woman who could chug a six-pack. Nervous energy was all that sustained her at the moment.

"What was it like?"

"What was what like?"

She held up a hand and twisted it back and forth in the

air, the fingers curved into a hook. She even pincered her thumb and index finger apart and back together.

"You'd have to ask Jana. She's the one it happened to."

"No, I mean…" Then she grimaced to herself. "I don't know what I mean."

"You mean, you've had too much beer."

"Or too little sleep. Your sister seems to think you're bothering me."

"Me?" He'd been damned careful to steer clear of her. Being around Stacy was like a constant adrenaline high. First he'd been taken by her beauty and sass. Then her piloting—because, damn, this woman could fly. Even his sister had remarked on it. Stacy also appeared to be the first woman friend Jana had chosen in a long time which was rare praise indeed. "How am I bothering you?"

"I don't know. I was thinking maybe you could tell me. I guess we'll never know." She unleashed a tonsil-deep yawn, then her head began sinking toward the last half of her beer and the last slice of pizza.

"Hold on a second." He waved a hand and got Jana's attention over at the pool table. He pointed at Jasper and made a key starting a car motion. Jana asked him something.

Jasper raised his head just enough to glare across the room at him from beneath the brim of his hat. A brief nod —yes, he did have his copy of the Firebird's key with him —then he returned to setting up his shot.

Curt didn't have to carry Stacy out to her truck—quite. Tucking her into the passenger seat almost undid him, though. The first brush of his fingers across her hair as he reached for her seatbelt was the first time he'd ever touched her in any way. *So that's what they mean by soft as silk.* He was careful not to touch her more than necessary as he reached across to buckle her in.

He suddenly couldn't remember if women wore seatbelts under their breasts, between them, or above them. After standing still for a long moment trying to figure it out, he tugged out all of the slack, snapped the buckle into the receiver, then let the retractor pull the seatbelt into the proper place on its own. Between their breasts. Good to know.

She was silent for the entire drive back to the field.

He made a point of releasing her buckle before he climbed out of her truck so that he wouldn't have to reach across her again. To his surprise, when he opened the passenger door, she clambered out. The only light was a distant security light, a sliver of a moon, and the stars.

"You know," she leaned back against her truck. "I think I figured out why you bother me."

"Do tell," he stood in front of her and admired how she looked in the dim light. Soft, real, and still a hundred percent herself. She belonged in her skin like no one he'd ever met. So sure of everything.

"That. Right there."

"What?"

"Well…just look at yourself."

"Hello. It's dark out and I don't have a mirror."

"I don't have one either, Mr. Curt-the-Huskies-fan, but I could describe you with my eyes closed."

"They already are," he teased her even though he could just make out glints of starlight reflections caught by them.

"Feet apart," her voice sounded as dreamy as the night. "Like Paul Bunyan standing in the forest. Arms folded over your chest like a guy on the defense even though he has no reason to be. And I'd wager that you're squinting at me like I've lost my mind."

"Well, you missed that entirely."

"How?"

"My feet are planted so that I don't come any closer. My arms are crossed in an attempt to keep my hands to myself. And my eyes are wide open, because you are a vision in the nighttime. Or in the air. Or—" Shit! He was the one who was supposed to be sober. How had he just said all those things to Stacy Richardson?

"Oh," her voice was almost as soft as the night.

"Oh?"

"Yes, oh."

Now he did squint at her, trying to see her expression, but there wasn't enough light.

"Why?"

"Why? I already told you why." And if this conversation went on any longer he was going to lose his mind.

"No, I mean why are you doing all those things rather than kissing me?"

He looked up at the stars for guidance and didn't find any.

"Maybe that's what's bothering me. You're awfully attractive, Curt Williams, except for your choice in football teams. I'm quite surprised to discover that I like you. And—"

"You're exhausted and you're drunk and I don't take advantage of women in altered states. Besides, I'm your boss."

"I'm tired and I nursed the same half beer for two hours. Probably more sober than you are."

"I'm still your boss. I'm not going to take advantage of you."

"Curious," she tipped her head to the side. "Makes me appreciate that bolt of integrity you wear like a sheriff's badge all the more. What happens if *I* decide to take advantage of *you?*"

Curt blew out a breath in exasperation, "How the hell should I know?"

"Hmm. Let's find out."

9

Stacy stepped into his arms—into his *crossed* arms, because she'd gotten that part right in the darkness. She had to rise up on her toes to kiss him due to the additional separation. For a long moment he didn't react…then she felt his smile against her lips. It was only there for a moment, but she found it very encouraging.

"You sure, Stacy?"

In answer she rested her hands on his arms and pulled them down, not releasing his wrists until they were headed around her and she could step the rest of the way against his chest.

Through his sister, he had promised her a challenging job, and he'd delivered. With the amazing quality of the Firebirds' fleet and hiring a mechanic with Maggie's skills, he'd promised safety. And for not being a total guy jerk—actually, not being one at all—*that* swept her feet right out from under her.

Then there was the kiss. His arms slid around her like they belonged and he eased her in against a chest that felt every bit as wonderful as it looked.

A part of her argued that this was a dumb idea because hadn't she just this evening told her friends that she wasn't interested in any men? Okay, maybe she hadn't told them, but she'd thought it really hard.

For all his macho and firefighter ego, he kissed like a movie-screen lover—long, slow, and perfect. On further testing, he was better than that because he was so impossibly real.

At length she sighed and lay her head on his shoulder as he toyed with her hair.

"You taste incredible."

"Like beer and pizza. I know what a man likes."

His chuckle rippled between them. "Like a dark mystery and the fresh air just rolling in off the wide ocean."

"Keep it up, Husky Boy," Stacy nuzzled in. She could happily go to sleep right here in his arms. "Don't stop and I'll drag you off into the tall grass."

He huffed out a breath against the top of her head like he'd just been sucker punched. It had been a while and she'd forgotten how easy it was to do that to a guy.

She shifted enough to hear his heartbeat and sighed happily. It *was* a perfect place to curl up and disappear.

"I found Stacy in her bed...alone." Jana found him sitting on the edge of one of the helicopter trailers. "What's up with that, C? Want to talk about it?"

"She fell asleep standing in my arms, J. I carried her in." She'd felt so light yet so substantial. If he'd had a bunk of his own, he might have carried her there. No. No, he wouldn't. But he certainly liked the idea. Maybe he should hurry up fixing the next bunkhouse.

Jana hiked herself up to sit on the trailer beside him. Out of habit, he gave her a hand to provide stability that her hooks didn't offer. That reminded him of Stacy's question.

"What was it like, J? Losing that." He tapped a finger on the plastic socket piece of her prosthetic.

"Seems like a distant dream now. Mostly I remember that it hurt like a son of a bitch. Looking back, I'd say I'm just glad it wasn't my head."

"If it had been, you'd have been fine. You're as hardheaded as I am. But that's not what I mean," Curt almost laughed. It was exactly what Stacy had said, but never clarified. "Guess I'm asking what's it like now?"

He could feel her scowl for a long time before she answered.

"You mean knowing that I'll never be whole again? Knowing that any guy I'd want to take to bed is going to be thoroughly grossed out when faced with a stub of a forearm rather than a hand? Like that?"

"Aww, shit, J." Curt looped an arm around her shoulders and pulled her in.

"That the only guy willing to touch you without judgement is a side hug from your little brother?" Her voice cracked hard and he held her tighter as she cleared her throat a couple times.

"I'm so sorry, J. I didn't realize. We're gonna have to find you a guy who isn't a dope."

"Good luck with that," she was back under tight control and sat up straight. He dropped his hand back to his lap. "Been three years. Why ask now?"

"Stacy asked and I didn't know the answer."

"Huh," Jana didn't sound pleased.

Stacy focused on the Brookfield Fire. It was a beast that had swept down out of the Ochoco National Forest, destroyed everything along Brookfield Lane in Prineville, Oregon almost before the alarm was sounded. It had already made authorities issue an evacuation order for a whole section of town. A dozen homes were already gone and a new neighborhood was under direct threat.

Assets were pouring in, but they were focused on blocking the heart of the fire that was headed straight for town. The new developments that had been spreading out north and east of the town were wide open. And there wasn't a whole lot of water in the arid countryside. All of the water was pumped out for irrigation of the broad fields, but was little help to their current situation. The nearest open water was the Barnes Butte Reservoir and it was so busy already with tanker aircraft that it was an air traffic control nightmare.

"That reservoir is a five minute round trip away!" Jasper complained over the Firebirds' private frequency from his MD 520N.

"Well, I'm not real happy about it either," Curt had replied from his own helo.

Most of the swimming pools were shaded by trees that wouldn't allow them to approach close enough without risking catching a rotor. With a rotor disc that swept less than thirty feet, she still couldn't find…

No. There!

"Next neighborhood to the west. I've got two pools with new trees. Maybe we can get in there." She didn't wait for anyone to acknowledge, she twisted her helo into a sharp dive and pulled up hard fifty feet over the first pool. She needed to get down below fifteen feet to dip her dangling snorkel hose into the water—ten was better. That would place her main rotor at seventeen feet above the ground.

There was one tree that was just too tall and close to the pool. It would be too risky to catch her tail rotor. Wait. This was a NOTAR helicopter. Having no tail rotor hadn't mattered at any time in the prior firefights, but her tailboom stuck six feet past the edge of the main rotor disc —so, unlike a conventional tail rotor, the NOTAR's tail could brush the trees and her main rotor would be safely in the clear.

The only problem was that she couldn't see it because it was directly behind her.

"Curt, spot my tail boom."

"You gotta kidding me."

Stacy wasn't, so she began settling down toward the swimming pool as Curt called distances. She liked his voice in her ears, like when he'd whispered in her ear at night.

They'd woken to a fire call the next day after their first kiss. But he hadn't protested when she'd dragged him into her tent that night. He was as self-assured a lover as he was a pilot. And every bit of that ego was deserved—he was the best lover she'd ever had and Stacy did her best to return the same.

"Fifteen feet," he called over the radio from where he hovered to one side for a clear view.

Thoughtful, considerate, and with a body that a woman could gladly wear herself out getting to know. They'd been cohabiting for a month, often too tired to do more than collapse together, but the nights they were awake for more were notably spectacular. There'd been the night camped along a remote curve in the wilderness along the Rogue River.

"Ten."

She continued easing down and released the snorkel. She leaned her head out into the bubble window mounted in the pilot's side door. The acrylic was bowed outward so that she could look directly down.

"Still ten."

That's how she rated Curt as well. A month together and still a ten. Unheard of in her experience. Last week they had flown into one of the hundreds of coves along the Oregon Coast only accessible by boat or helicopter. For two glorious days they hadn't even bothered with clothes, making love on the pale sand with only seagulls, sandpipers, and a rather curious seal out in the surf looking on. A powerful man's naked body lit only by a beach campfire as he'd grilled salmon had been a revelation.

"Five. I don't like this, Stacy."

But he wasn't calling her off yet and she continued descending. She spied along the snorkel and shifted closer to the edge of the pool away from the trees. Her rotor's downwash blew aside lawn furniture and scattered pool tools. The owner, who should already have evacuated, stood on his rear deck yelling at her and shaking his fist.

He was more worried about the neatness of his lawn than the fast approaching wildfire.

"Back up to eight with that last move."

The way they moved together was pure magic. Their bodies finding rhythms that echoed far deeper than merely a happy nervous system. The synchronicity was tighter than between an intermeshing rotor system. Except she had no tail rotor. It should be disorienting. Instead, she felt clearer than she ever had before in her life.

The snorkel hit the water five feet from the pool's edge, she eased forward another three feet. The owner had retreated to glower through his sliding glass door.

"Ten or eleven," Curt called out.

Stacy hit the pump switch and the belly tank that hung between her skids began filling.

"Okay, listen up. My alignment points are the swim ladder exactly bracketing a gate in the fence. That will give us ten feet of tail clearance. We're less than a thirty-second flight from the fire. That means that three of us can work this pool. Come in, load up, fly out to deliver as the next one round-robins down to fill. See if we can do that at the other pool."

"On it," Jasper called just as her tank hit full and she eased up and out.

Damn but she loved flying these aircraft. The Firebirds totally rocked.

---

*C*urt came dropping in close behind her. Amos hovered in turn and began calling Curt's tail clearances—they stayed above ten feet the whole way using Stacy's guideposts.

Within minutes they had two three-helicopter rotations gulping up and delivering two hundred-gallon loads of water in a near continuous stream. That was as fast as most fire trucks could deliver it—except the trucks had already been ordered to fall back a street and were no longer on the front line.

One by one they chopped gaps in the fire with their helos—down to the pool, pump, up even as Amos' bird came down, follow Stacy to the fire, dump on the burning trees and lawn, turn back to pool, down as she once more lifted away. They herded the flames through vacant lots where the firefighters on the ground had set up wet lines and were pumping for all they were worth.

It was like a dream, following in Stacy's wake. That's how it felt being with her. He'd always thought of himself as the leader type—the Firebirds had been his initial idea.

But he couldn't keep up with Stacy. In the air, she was magnificent, and on the ground... His body was still tingling with the memory of her running wild on the beach. She'd raced laps along the wet sand which stretched a half mile end-to-end, dressed in only a sports bra, sunglasses, and tennis shoes. Like a goddess Venus in dog tags risen from the waves for his own private delight.

She never spoke about those dog tags, even though they'd often been the only thing she wore. He'd read the name. She'd lost a husband in one of the wars. That had to be some bad pain and he was careful not to bring it up.

The pools were running dry by the time they had this section of the fire beaten without a single house lost. Though Curt was glad he wouldn't have to face the owner of the empty pool—he was still giving them a dirty look out the back window every time he tanked up.

"Refuel," he ordered the team. Hover-and-lift burned the Jet Fuel A fast. And with a whole neighborhood secured it was time for them to get down and take a break as well.

Jana had a helispot set up at a scenic viewpoint on the far side of town, just a few minutes' flight away.

Once more he was following Stacy like a hungry dog who couldn't get enough. And he knew he never would, not given a dozen years to try, or a hundred.

There was a startling thought. A lifetime? Could he have found his lifetime lady? He'd never really expected to. Oh, he'd find someone to settle down with someday, but there wasn't time in his life to do the finding. He was maxed out with keeping the business afloat. They were doing well, but the season was far from break-even still. An early end to the fire season could still kill them off far too easily.

He didn't want the distraction of a relationship. It

didn't matter that she made him feel smarter, stronger, better than he knew he was. A relationship right now would be a pain in the ass.

That had him chuckling to himself as he settled down in Ochoco Wayside State Park just north of a bright green golf course, so well irrigated that there wasn't a chance of it burning. The wayside was a parched area of browning grasses and thirty-foot Douglas fir and larch scattered about. But the viewpoint itself was a paved loop with enough room to safely land their six Firebirds. Jana had parked the service and transport vehicles along the entry road and set up camp while they'd been fighting the fire.

Pain in the ass. That's how Stacy Richardson had introduced herself. The only pain she gave him was when they weren't side by side.

He fell in beside her as they crossed over to where the ground team had set up a lunch spread for the pilots.

"You're gonna marry me when this is all over, right?" He tried to make it sound like a joke at the end, because he sure as hell hadn't meant to say it from the beginning. Marriage? Shit, no!

"Sure," he was glad her tone was light—lighter than his. "Just as soon I can think of any reason that I'd want to."

Curt grabbed her hand to stop her. She looked at him in surprise, but he held his silence until the other pilots had moved by them at Cruise Speed (max) toward the picnic table.

"There's going to be a reason, isn't there?" He asked as soon as they were alone. He hadn't meant to sound so serious—was surprised to discover that he was.

She reached out and brushed a thumb down his cheek.

Turning his head into her hand he was able to leave a kiss in her palm.

"Been practicing that romantic approach for a while, have you?" Her smile said that she knew he'd blurted it out without intending to.

"I…know how to fly." How to deal with the woman looking up at him with those warm brown eyes was beyond him.

Then he saw a hint of sadness in her eyes and he didn't like where that was leading at all. He wanted to turn his good ear toward her and ask again because he couldn't be hearing this properly…but there was nothing wrong with his vision.

She brushed her thumb down his cheek again, then followed the others to the table.

Jana was headed the other way to join Maggie in checking over the helos and making sure they were ready to go aloft again. His sister had cooled toward Stacy at the same rate that he'd been heating up. His sister was the best judge of people he'd ever met, but she was wrong this time.

"Trouble in paradise, C?" Jana said as she passed him.

"Eat hot shit, J!"

She stumbled to a halt and turned back to look at him. "Rattlesnake bite you?"

He glared at her.

"Look, Curt," it was never a good sign when she used his full name. "I've got some issues with her, but they're mine. Don't let them affect you."

"What issues? She's amazing."

"In bed, I'm sure." Jana grimaced an apology. "There's something hidden in her and I don't trust it. She's damaged goods and I know what I'm talking about." She raised her hooks to emphasize her point.

He'd forgotten about the night Stacy had asked him about Jana's artificial hand. It had been a strange thing to do and he remembered it gut-punching his sister when he'd related the story later that night.

"She ever mention it?" he asked, nodding toward her hand.

"Not a word, not a glance. You two have been shacking up, so I only see her on the flight line or at meals, but there's something about it that bothers her in a weird way."

At his silence, Jana shrugged and moved off.

Curt knew he wasn't the deepest thinker, but Jana's caution had kicked him into high gear—or at least a higher one than usual. Jana's radar about people was always spot on. His was okay with guys, but lousy with women.

Was Stacy backing away because he had a handicapped sister? That didn't sound right. If it wasn't that, he didn't know what it could be. He could try asking, but some part of that higher thinking gear warned him that he might not like the answer—like probing a sore tooth until it was screaming.

13

*S*tacy couldn't believe it. How could something so good become so screwed up in a single week? By the time they left the fire in Prineville, Curt had been growing distant. Jasper, of course, picked up on it right away and began avoiding her as well. Between one moment and the next, she'd become the rotting jellyfish on the beach.

Back at their Illinois Valley Airport base, the nerves had caught up with her in the middle of the night. She'd slipped out of Curt's bed and headed out into the dark. She couldn't exactly move back in with the girls—Jana had made it clear that she wanted nothing to do with her.

At a loss for where else to go, she climbed into the back of her pickup, leaving the cap's tail flap up so that she could see the stars.

It was too familiar. Too real.

She and her brother had camped together in this truck —a lot. They'd had to leave the tailgate down, even in the rain, because Bill's legs had been too long for the short bed. They'd scrunch up together, pressed shoulder-to-shoulder by the wheel wells intruding from either side and tell stories and make up jokes. After he'd joined the Army, they'd spent almost all of his leaves out camping. Then he'd told her everything he could about flight operations.

Now she huddled alone in the dark, lying on the truck bed, clutching her fist around the dog tags that were the most prized vestiges of Bill's life: the last thing to have touched him that she had. The dog tags that Curt had never asked about. There was no going home. If she went back to the family farm, she'd never leave.

Instead, she'd rot there just like her parents and never—

"He throw you out?"

Stacy yelped in surprise at hearing Jana's voice echo inside the truck's cap. She could make out Jana's silhouette where she'd leaned her crossed arms on the tailgate.

"Sorry to have spooked you."

"You don't sound it."

The shadow shrugged.

"No, I left on my own. He was sleeping."

It earned her a Williams family trademark grunt.

"I thought you weren't talking to me."

Again the shrug. "You've got him pretty screwed up. Figured I'd ask why. You having fun doing that to my brother?"

"No!" It burst out of her without thought or pretense. "I am?" She hated how that felt.

There was an odd sound that Stacy couldn't figure out at first. Like someone tapping their fingers together…if they were made of steel and rubber.

"I don't intend to be. But I can't marry him."

"Marriage?" Now it was Jana's turn for an outburst. "My idiot brother proposed to you?"

"Sort of… Not really. But maybe…"

"When?"

"The day of the fire in Prineville, after we did the swimming pool trick."

"I reviewed the footage on that. That was some ace work. Really first-skill flight."

"Thanks. I guess."

"Do you mind?" Then without waiting for an answer, Jana lowered the tailgate and sat down on it.

Not wanting to talk to Jana's back, Stacy scooted forward until they were sitting side by side, dangling their feet off the end as if neither of them was willing to jump into the swimming hole.

Jana was the first to break the silence. "Why did you want to know what it was like to lose my hand?"

"I didn't. Don't. It must have been awful."

"My asshole brother says you did."

"No, I..." Stacy had the nasty feeling that she was finished with this outfit. For a brief moment in time, she'd thought she'd found somewhere to be. Flying to fire, in a helicopter with her very own name on it, an amazing lover, but... "I wanted to know what it was like *for him* to almost lose his sister. I shouldn't have asked."

"Why did you?"

Stacy tried to think about how to not answer that question, but wasn't having much luck. Jana was in her scary-interviewer mode and it was definitely working.

"This truck belonged to my brother. He was all that saved me from my life. From my past."

"But you have it now."

"But I have it now. He flew for the Night Stalkers."

That earned her a low whistle of respect. "Where is he now?"

"In an urn of ash buried beneath a cross at Arlington Cemetery. Better than Otis, I suppose."

Jana's silence let Stacy slowly tell the rest of the story about home, and flying, even her foolish dreams of flying with her brother in the Army someday.

"I couldn't face the Army after he died. So, I flew to fire instead. Swore I'd never marry a pilot. Curt slipped past my guard. I wasn't even aware of it until he made that joke about marriage. Then I knew that I had no choice. I love flying with the Firebirds and my brother taught me to fly an MD 500, so the 520 is like coming home. But I can't marry a pilot."

Jana was silent for so long that Stacy was starting to wonder if she'd ever speak to her again. There was enough time for most of Orion's belt to move from one side of a treetop to another.

"Jana?"

"I'm just trying to decide which of the three of us is stupidest here."

"Stupid?"

"Maybe thoughtless is a better word."

"I'm not a big fan of either one."

"Doesn't surprise me, Stacy. That's one of the things I liked about you in that first interview. Smart woman who was on her toes. The thing is, I think we've all screwed up in this case."

"Might as well tell me, because I can't feel any worse at the moment."

"Me first." Jana tapped her hooks on the tailgate loudly enough to startle Stacy. "Because I thought you were being typically ghoulish about my amputation, I dumped you into my not-worth-wasting-my-time-with pile. The fact that you started screwing my brother the next night just confirmed that you were a first-class bitch."

"Usually I'm called a pain in the ass. And I started

screwing him, because he's the nicest and best man I've ever met."

"Was that opinion before or after he took you to bed? No, don't answer. If you were in the running, you'd never make more than second-class bitch in this outfit, because I'm gonna win that first prize any day of the week."

Stacy found herself smiling at Jana's dry tone. It felt more like that night they'd sung songs together on the way to the Cave Junction pizza joint.

"My brother—who I love dearly, don't get me wrong— is about as deep as a mud puddle. He's a good guy, but if you're going to marry him, just accept that if you want him to know something, you're gonna have to tell him. Directly, in simple words. He'll never think to ask."

"But I'm not—"

"Number Three of this screwed up trio is you. Why the hell *wouldn't* you want to marry a heli-pilot? Nobody else is ever going to meet our standards. We're heli-women of the Firebirds. There's nothing better than us and we deserve the same."

Stacy didn't know what to say to that. Had she somehow had it backwards all this time? Her brother had been a helicopter pilot, and he was the best man she'd ever known.

And Curt? After such a short time together, Curt was already at a tie with Bill in her heart. What would he be with more time? Would he be even more than she thought he was? Even better than he already…

She ran out of steam. Sitting here on the back of her brother's old truck—less than a hundred feet from the bed she'd left Curt in—and she missed him like he was a thousand miles away. Curt Williams wasn't a part of her thoughts, he was a part of her very breath.

"Hey."

Stacy startled. Curt was standing only a few steps in front of her. She turned, but Jana was gone and Stacy didn't know for how long. Long enough for Orion to move fully clear of the treetop and for Canis Major, his loyal dog, to start the transition.

"Hey yourself." *Brilliant response, Stacy.*

"I woke up and I missed you."

"You found me." She hoped that it was a good sign that he even wanted to.

"Let me guess. You're sitting here in the middle of the night, thinking about how to tell me you're going to finally upgrade this old thing for a nice new Chevy Camaro ZL1."

Jana was right. Curt Williams was a very straight-ahead guy, but he was also such a good one. To offer a tease despite everything else that had happened between them these last days. She couldn't imagine finding anyone better. Ever.

"If I ever do, I'm having it painted Oregon Duck green and yellow."

"You wouldn't!" he sounded aghast.

Then, in a very different tone. One full of the night and just the two of them, he asked softly.

"You okay?"

She reached out and found his hand, then tugged him toward her. Stacy pulled him in until she lay her ear on his heart and wrapped her arms around his waist.

Slowly, ever so slowly, he wrapped his arms around her in answer.

Yes, she was okay. With Curt to ground her and keep her sane, she could finally be okay.

But for him? Then she smiled and turned her nose into his sternum. He'd already made his choice. Next time he gave voice to it, she wouldn't be stupid or thoughtless.

Neither would she hesitate. Though there wasn't a chance he was going to make her trade in her pickup on a muscle car.

Other than that, for as long as they were together, they'd most certainly be flying.

FIRE LIGHT, FIRE BRIGHT (EXCERPT)

IF YOU LIKED THIS, YOU'LL LOVE THE HOTSHOT SHORT STORIES!

FIRE LIGHT, FIRE BRIGHT

(EXCERPT)

"Hi, I'm Candace Cantrell. First Rule: anyone who calls me Candy, who isn't my dad," she hooked a thumb at Fire Chief Carl Cantrell standing at-ease beside her, "is gonna get my boot up their ass. We clear on that?"

A rolling mumble of "Yes, ma'am." "Clear." and "Got it, Candace." rippled back to her from the recruits. Some answered almost as softly as the breeze working its way up through the tall pines. Others trumpeting it out as if to get her notice. A few offered simple nods.

She surveyed the line of recruits slowly. Way too early to make any judgments, but it was tempting. Day One, Minute One, and she could already guess five of the forty applicants weren't going to make it into the twenty slots she had open.

The one thing they all, including her dad, needed to see right up front was their team leader's complete confidence. Candace had been fighting wildfires for the U.S. Forest Service hotshot teams for a decade. She'd worked her way up to foreman twice, and had been gunning for a shot at superintendent of a whole twenty-person crew when her dad had called.

"We're got permission to form up an IHC in the heart of the Okanagan-Wenatchee National Forest," he never was long on greetings over the phone.

Her mouth had watered. A brand new Interagency Hotshot Crew didn't happen all that often.

"I talked to the other captains and we want you to form it up."

Now her throat had gone dry and she had to fight to not let it squeak.

"Me?"

"You aren't gonna let me down now, Candy Girl?"

"You shittin' me?" Not a chance.

Then he'd hit her with that big belly laugh of his.

"Knew you'd like the idea."

And simple as that, she'd been out of the San Juan IHC at the end of the Colorado fire season and back home in the Cascade Mountains of Washington State. She'd grown up in the resort town of Leavenworth—two thousand people and a ka-jillion tourists. The city fathers had transformed the failing timber town into a Bavarian wonderland back in the sixties. But that didn't stop the millions of acres of the National Forest and the rugged sagebrush-steppe ecosystem further east in central Washington from torching off every summer.

The very first thing she'd done, before she'd even left the San Juan IHC, was to call in a pair of ringers as her two foremen. Jess was short, feisty, and could walk up forested mountains all day with heavy gear without slowing down a bit. Patsy was tall, quiet, and tough. Candace had them stand in with the candidates for the first days because she wanted their eyes out there as well.

"Second, see that road?" she asked the recruits and

pointed to the foot of National Forest Road 6500. She'd had their first meet-up be here rather than at the fire hall in town. A gaggle of vehicles were pulled off the dirt of Little Wenatchee River Road. Beater pickups dominated, but there were a couple of hammered Civics, a pair of muscle cars, and a gorgeous Harley Davidson that she considered stealing it was so sweet.

The recruits all looked over their shoulders at the one lane of dirt.

"We're going for a stroll up that road. We leave in sixty seconds."

Like a herd of sheep, they all swung their heads to look at her.

"Fifty-five seconds, and this ain't gonna be a Sunday-type of a stroll."

You could tell the number of seasons they'd fought fire just by their reactions.

Five or more? They already wore their boots. Daypacks with water and energy bars were kept on their shoulders during her intro. And despite it being Day One of the ten-day shakedown, all had some tools: fold-up shovel and a heavy knife strapped to their leg at a minimum. Only she, Jess, and Patsy had Pulaski wildland fire axes tied to their gear, but all the veterans knew the drill.

Three to four seasons? Groans and eyerolls. Packs were on the ground beside them. No tools, but they knew what was coming now that she'd told them—ten kilometers, at least, and not one meter of it flat.

One to two seasons? Had the right boots on, but no packs. They were racing back to their vehicles to see what equipment they could assemble.

Rookies? Tennis shoes, ball caps, no gear, blank stares.

"Forty-five seconds, rooks. Boots and water. If you're

not on the trail in fifty seconds, you're off the crew." That got their asses moving.

There was one man on the whole crew she couldn't pigeonhole, the big guy who'd climbed off the Harley. His pack and the fold-up shovel strapped to it were so new they sparkled. But his boots and the massive hunting knife on his thigh both showed very heavy use.

A glance at her Dad's assessing gaze confirmed it. Something was odd about the Harley man and his easy grin. Not rugged handsome, but still very nice to look at. Powerful shoulders, slim waist. Not an athlete's build, but rather someone who really used his body. His worn jeans revealed that he already had the powerful legs that every hotshot would develop from endless miles of chasing fire over these mountains and steppes for the next six months. It was like he was a Hollywood movie: some parts of him were so very right, but a lot of the details were dead wrong.

***

Luke Rawlings looked at the team superintendent. Couldn't help himself, 'cause damn she was a treat to look at. Her white-blond hair was short and sassy, her body was seriously fit, but curved like a sweet-Candy dream girl. Her no-nonsense attitude just cracked him up; he could hear that natural state of command that you only learned the hard way, by doing it. Not something he'd ever expected to find in a hot civilian babe.

When he'd mustered out, SEAL Lieutenant Commander Altman had suggested he try firefighting. Altman was a smart dude, so Luke had followed his suggestion. He'd kicked around with a big city fire department doing ride-alongs for a while. Chicago Fire were all super guys and they kept trying to sign him aboard, but tramping pavement and cement, doing fire inspections for date tags on commercial fire extinguishers…he'd rather be back in the African jungle. If his nerves would let him, which he so wasn't going to think about now.

He still wasn't sure how he'd heard about the hotshot crews, but walking into a wildfire—he just liked the way it sounded.

And looking at "Not Candy" Cantrell, he was damn glad he'd followed his whim and ridden his Harley west.

Available at fine retailers everywhere!
Fire Light, Fire Bright

ABOUT THE AUTHOR

M.L. Buchman started the first of, what is now over 50 novels and as many short stories, while flying from South Korea to ride his bicycle across the Australian Outback. Part of a solo around the world trip that ultimately launched his writing career.

All three of his military romantic suspense series—The Night Stalkers, Firehawks, and Delta Force—have had a title named "Top 10 Romance of the Year" by the American Library Association's *Booklist.* NPR and Barnes & Noble have named other titles "Top 5 Romance of the Year." In 2016 he was a finalist for Romance Writers of America prestigious RITA award. He also writes: contemporary romance, thrillers, and fantasy.

Past lives include: years as a project manager, rebuilding and single-handing a fifty-foot sailboat, both flying and jumping out of airplanes, and he has designed and built two houses. He is now making his living as a full-time writer on the Oregon Coast with his beloved wife and is constantly amazed at what you can do with a degree in Geophysics. You may keep up with his writing and receive a free starter e-library by subscribing to his newsletter at: www.mlbuchman.com

Other works by M. L. Buchman:

www.ingramcontent.com/pod-product-compliance
Lightning Source LLC
Chambersburg PA
CBHW051713180726
48283CB00004B/1325